Changes, Changes

By PAT HUTCHINS

THE BODLEY HEAD
LONDON · SYDNEY · TORONTO

ISBN 0 370 01548 7
Copyright © Pat Hutchins 1971
Printed Offset Litho in Great Britain for
The Bodley Head Ltd
9 Bow Street, London WC2E 7AL
By Cox & Wyman Ltd, Fakenham
Published in New York by The Macmillan Company, 1971
First published in Great Britain 1971

For Elsie and Bob Bruce